MW01195972

The Adventures of Onyx
and
The Saginaw River Ice Rescuers

by Tyler Benson

Ensign Benson Books LLC

Ensign Benson Books LLC
www.adventuresofonyx.com
ensignbensonbooks@gmail.com

Printed and bound in China

First Edition

10 9 8 7 6 5 4 3 2

LCCN 2016914690

ISBN 978-0-9892846-8-4

book bridge press sm

This book was expertly produced by Book Bridge Press.
www.bookbridgepress.com

One of my favorite quotes by Mark Twain is "The two most important days in your life are the day you are born and the day you find out why." Thank you to two of my mentors, Mike Hudson and Keith Bills, for helping me discover my purpose and passion to teach others, and to add value to other peoples' lives.

—Tyler

"Training time-out!" Petty Officer Abold called.

Onyx and the Guardians of the Straits quickly gathered around their lead ice rescue instructor. They were training at the Coast Guard's National Ice Rescue School.

"It's time for your final test," Abold said. "Coast Guard Station Saginaw River needs our help. They have received two separate emergency calls about people who have fallen through the ice in Saginaw Bay. The station is responding to the first emergency, and I have been directed to build a crew and launch for the second emergency. You all have proven to be my most skilled ice rescue students this week, and I believe you can get the job done. Who is with me?"

Dean looked at Evans, Hogan, and Onyx. Then he nodded to Abold and said, "Lead the way. We are ready!"

Abold nodded back. "Good," he said. "Then you are no longer my students. You are Saginaw River Ice Rescuers!"

Onyx barked excitedly for her new adventure.

"So what is the emergency?" Hogan asked.

"A man and snowmobile have crashed through the ice about a mile out in Saginaw Bay," Abold said. "Coast Guard Station Saginaw River has directed the launch of our ice rescue team aboard our airboat, and an aircrew from the Coast Guard Air Station has been requested to back us up. We will take the station's truck and tow the airboat over to the bay. Then we will launch in the airboat from the closest point to the snowmobiler in distress."

Dean, Hogan, Evans, and Abold did not waste any time. They suited up in their ice rescue suits and ran with Onyx to the truck.

The Saginaw River Ice Rescuers sped down the snow-covered road with their airboat in tow. Hogan pulled Onyx's seatbelt tighter. Abold concentrated on the road, gripping the steering wheel as he carefully wove in and out of traffic.

"Hang on," Abold called out. "Every second counts. Depending on what that snowmobiler is wearing, he might not last long in the bitter cold waters of Saginaw Bay. Cold water can kill."

"You don't have to explain it to us," Evans said. "Just keep going!"

Onyx barked in agreement.

Within minutes, the Saginaw River Ice Rescuers pulled into a state park next to Saginaw Bay where local firefighters were waiting. Hogan, Onyx, and Evans were out the door before the truck came to a full stop.

"Nice driving!" Dean said.

"You haven't seen anything yet!" Abold replied. "Now let's hurry and get this airboat off the trailer."

Evans grabbed a lever on the trailer and yelled, "Clear!"

Onyx stood by as the trailer lifted and the airboat quickly slid off onto the snow.

"Gear up, team!" Dean called. "We need to launch in the next three minutes."

"Onyx, I have something for you!" Abold said and ran back over to the truck.

Onyx watched Abold pull some gear from the truck then hurry back. He kneeled down beside Onyx and placed new ice rescue headgear and goggles on her.

"There you go, girl," Abold said, petting Onyx on the head. "Ice rescue is dangerous work in the harshest conditions. Every little piece of gear can help!"

Onyx barked excitedly and wagged her tail.

"All right, then. We're ready!" Abold yelled. "Let's go to work!"

Abold and Dean climbed into the front seat of the airboat, and Evans, Hogan, and Onyx climbed into the back. Suddenly the whistle of a Coast Guard helicopter could be heard overhead.

Hogan looked up and said, "There she is! There is Pelkey and her Angels in the Air!"

"Awesome!" Dean said. "The team is back together. Now let's get out there and do what we do best, save lives!"

Onyx barked and Abold fired up the engine. The airboat fan began to spin faster and faster, and the entire airboat began to vibrate. Abold gave a thumbs-up to his team.

Dean looked back at Onyx and yelled, "Coming up!"

Abold put the throttle down and the Saginaw River Ice Rescuers launched into action onto ice-covered Saginaw Bay.

The airboat quickly moved across the ice. "Abold!" Hogan yelled over the engine noise. "How many of these calls do you get a year?"

"This time of year the ice is extremely unpredictable," Abold said. "We do our best to educate people about the dangers of venturing out onto the thinning ice as winter transitions into spring, but we still get lots of calls about people in trouble."

"How many?" Hogan asked again.

"The Coast Guard responds to an average of 100 ice rescues per year around all of the Great Lakes," Abold said. "Coast Guard Station Saginaw River is involved in about twenty-five of those cases."

Hogan looked at Onyx and shook his head in amazement. "I take it that is why the Coast Guard's National Ice Rescue School is here off of Saginaw Bay?" Hogan asked.

"You got that right!" Abold said.

Suddenly Dean shouted and pointed. "There he is! I've got eyes on our snowmobiler in distress."

Abold brought the airboat to a sliding stop.

"Everyone out!" Abold yelled. "It's time to go to work. It's time to save a life! Dean, you and Evans start setting up. Hogan, you make contact with the snowmobiler. I'll call it in to the station that we are on scene."

Dean quickly clipped himself up to the rescue board, and Evans screwed an ice anchor into the ice.

Hogan made his way toward the snowmobiler. "Sir, United States Coast Guard. We're here to help you. Keep holding onto the ice shelf. We're coming to save you as soon as we can."

"Help me!" the man screamed.

Hogan could hear the chattering of the man's teeth and see the blue in his face and lips. *We don't have much time,* Hogan thought. Just then, the ice beneath Hogan began to crack and then broke away from under his feet. Hogan fell through the ice, but caught himself before he went under.

"Hogan!" Dean yelled.

"I am all right!" Hogan called as he pulled himself back onto the ice. "You can't save others unless you know how to save yourself, right?" Hogan yelled back to his team.

"That ice is too weak for the weight of any of us," Hogan told the team. "If we try to approach the man, we will definitely break the ice shelf he is holding onto, and the weight of his wet clothes will send him to the bottom of Saginaw Bay."

"I'm radioing the helicopter to circle around," Abold said. "They can come in over him and lower the rescue swimmer."

"There is no time!" Hogan said. "I could see from his face that he is suffering from severe hypothermia. His body temperature has dropped too low and he is in and out of consciousness. He is going to let go of that ice shelf and sink long before the helo circles back around. We have to go now!"

"But, Hogan," Evans said, "that ice is too weak for any of our weight."

"You're right, Evans," Hogan replied, "but not for a miracle dog." Hogan unclipped Dean from the ice rescue board and kneeled down next to Onyx. "Go get him, Onyx," he said, and he clipped her up to the board. "Go save that man!"

Without hesitation Onyx ran across the ice for the man. She pulled the rescue board behind her.

As Onyx got closer to the man, the ice began to crack. Onyx stopped. She looked back at Hogan.

"What's the matter with her?" Dean asked. "I've never seen her like this."

"She's scared," Hogan replied.

"It must be because she saw you go through the ice," Dean said.

"No, it's something else. Things have been different with her since she had puppies last fall. She doesn't take the risks that she once did," Hogan said.

"That's it. Call in the helo," Dean said to Abold.

Hogan stepped forward and called to Onyx. "Onyx, listen to my voice. You can do this. You have survived heavy seas, gale force winds, waterfalls, and fire. You can brave the ice. That man needs you right now. This is what you were born to do, to be brave. Be brave!"

Onyx looked back and made eye contact with the man. "Help me, dog. Help me," the man whispered as he shivered uncontrollably.

Suddenly the ice shelf broke and the man went under the ice. Onyx sprinted across the ice and went in after him.

The rescue board went to the ice edge. Onyx and the man had disappeared beneath the ice.

"Onyx!" Hogan yelled.

"Heave around!" Abold yelled back to the team.

Hogan, Evans, and Dean pulled and pulled on the rescue line that was attached to Onyx and the rescue board, but she didn't come back up.

Abold radioed the Angels in the Air for help.

"Hook me up to another rescue line!" Hogan yelled. "She must be caught under the ice. I'm going after her!"

"Look!" Dean yelled.

Onyx had surfaced with the man. He grabbed hold of the rescue board as Onyx pulled herself with all her might back onto the ice.

"Onyx!" the Saginaw River Ice Rescuers cheered.

"Heave around!" Abold yelled as he jumped on the rescue line to pull the board to them.

Onyx ran alongside the man lying on the rescue board.

Hogan watched her run across the ice toward her team. "Shipmates, not heavy seas, not gale force winds, not strong currents or waterfalls, not blazing fires or ice could stop the heart of that dog from doing what she was born to do, to save lives. She's a miracle. She's truly a Coastie."

The Saginaw River Ice Rescuers quickly loaded the man into the airboat. He needed medical attention right away. His body temperature was dangerously low.

The man put his hand on Hogan's shoulder. "The dog, the dog. It risked its life for me. It's a miracle. It's a miracle," the man said.

"She sure is," Hogan replied and smiled. "And her name is Onyx." Hogan secured the man inside the airboat and gave Abold a thumbs-up. Abold fired up the airboat.

"Coming up!" Dean called out as the Saginaw River Ice Rescuers and Onyx made their way back toward shore.

Back at shore, Abold brought the airboat to a stop behind an ambulance awaiting their arrival. Emergency Medical Services quickly evaluated the snowmobiler for further treatment.

The Coast Guard helo landed in the park and powered down. Pelkey jumped out and ran over to the crew. "I was watching from the air," Pelkey said, "and I feared the worst there for a moment."

Hogan stepped over and put his hand on Onyx. "Onyx showed us today that bravery is not the absence of fear, but the victory over it." Hogan kneeled down next to the miracle dog, pulled her goggles and headgear off, and looked her in the eyes. "Your actions inspire us all. You are a miracle dog. You have proven yet again on another adventure that you are a brave Coastie."

Onyx barked and licked Hogan's face.

"And let's not forget," Abold announced, "you are also now a part of the Saginaw River Ice Rescuers."

GREAT LAKES AUTHOR **Tyler Benson** is from St. Louis, Michigan. He has served in the United States Coast Guard for more than a decade in St. Ignace, Michigan. He began writing short stories about his search-and-rescue adventures in the Coast Guard to educate his four young children about what Daddy does when he goes on duty for forty-eight hours at a time. He wanted them to learn the importance of service to their country  and helping those in need. To help them better understand his job, Tyler wrote the stories featuring his station's morale dog, Onyx. These stories soon evolved into a dream—to publish a book series that would serve as a tribute and a way to bring recognition to all who serve or have served in the United States Coast Guard.

The Saginaw River Ice Rescuers is Tyler's eighth book in the successful Adventures of Onyx series. Let the adventures continue!

www.adventuresofonyx.com